ABDO Publishing Company is the exclusive school and library distributor of Rabbit Ears Books.

Library bound edition 2005.

Library of Congress Cataloging-in-Publication Data

Kunstler, James Howard.
  Johnny Appleseed / written by James Howard Kunstler ; illustrated by Stan Olson.
    p. cm.
  Originally published: New York, NY : Rabbit Ears Books, 1995.
  ISBN 1-59197-765-7
  1. Appleseed, Johnny, 1774-1845—Juvenile literature. 2. Apple growers—United
States—Biography—Juvenile literature. 3. Frontier and pioneer life—Middle West—Juvenile
literature. I. Olson, Stan, ill. II. Title.

SB63.C46K86 2005
634'.11'092—dc22
[B]

                                                2004047697

All Rabbit Ears books are reinforced library binding
and manufactured in the United States of America.

ABDO
Publishing Company

WRITTEN BY
JAMES HOWARD KUNSTLER

Johnny
APPLESEED

ILLUSTRATED BY STAN OLSON

RABBIT EARS
BOOKS

Here was a sight to beat all: a man in the prime of life rambling barefoot down the wilderness road, dressed in raggedy pantaloons sewn out of two meal sacks, a shirt so tattered and scrappish that its owner had a proud choice of holes to stick his arms through, and—the crowning glory—a hat in the exact likeness of a tin mush pot, somewhat dented, but snugly fitted, with the handle turned to one side, as if it were the very latest and smartest of fashions.

Now, this odd duck's name was Jonathan Chapman. But along the Ohio, frontier folks called him Johnny Appleseed. The year was eighteen hundred and eleven. The place was a wilderness highway that the pioneers called Zane's Trace in the center of O-hi-o.

Johnny had a way of walking that was as queer as his costume. Slight as a picket, he marched down the trace upright, head held high, like a fusilier in the army. Only with every other footstep, his arms would flutter akimbo and fly up as though he was a great bird preparing to launch himself skyward.

As he marched and flapped, Johnny whistled a tune. Sometimes a quick and merry one like "Yankee Doodle," and other times it was haunting, lonesome, like a church hymn—which was another peculiar thing about this worthy fellow, for he knew how to whistle as many as three notes at once.

Now, on this particular day, Johnny was rambling from Guernsey County to a spot on the banks of the Muskingum River to inspect an orchard of Northern Spy apples that he had planted six years earlier. You see, Johnny had took upon himself the job of sowing apple trees in remote places all over the frontier. In fact, more than a job, it was his joy, his duty, his very reason for living. His young apple orchards were like a great welcome mat that he flung over Ohio for the settlers arriving and those yet to come. And he always remembered where he planted each and every one, like a father who knows where to look for each of his children.

This fine September afternoon the forest-clad hills were just beginning to blaze in fall's scarlet and coppery hues. Johnny marched along the trace—which was no more'n a rutted wagon trail—until he come upon a family of rattlesnakes sunning themselves on a stretch of flat rocks.

"Halloo thar, brother and sister snakes!" Johnny sang out, and doffed his mush pot.

The rattlers wagged their rattles as though they were pleased to see him.

Now, an ordinary frontiersman would have lowered his rifle and plugged them scaly varmints, but Johnny was not ordinary, and he carried no rifle or gun. He had a reverence for all life, be it as low and ugly as a sowbug or as fair as a child. To him, every walking, flying, swimming, creeping thing had the divine spark of life in it, and he would not harm it.

If a hornet flew into his raggedy pants, why Johnny just figured the poor thing was scared to find itself lost in such a deep dark cave, and he endured its stings until it departed. If he was fixing to sleep in the woods on a fall night, Johnny would rather lie in the cold than build a fire that might kill any of the season's last lingering mosquitoes.

As for the great beasts of the forest, the bears and wolves, they must have sensed that there was something different about Johnny, 'cause they always were friendly and obliging. The bears would rub their backs against him like he was their favorite back-scratching tree, and the wolves liked to lick his beard.

Anyway, on this particular fall day, Johnny sat down on the side of the road and sang hymns for the rattlesnakes till they had enough of it and slithered away.

Then he resumed marching until he came upon a spotted horse standing all by itself, no saddle nor harness nor any sign of its owner. It was a forlorn and wretched-looking mare, ribs poking against its hide like it hadn't eaten anything but weeds for a month, its eyes all red and rheumy like it had cried the whole time. And the poor thing was lame, too.

You see, it took a dreadful long journey to get out to Ohio from back East then. Sometimes, a horse or a cow got hurt along the way, and was no more use to the pioneer family that brought it, so they'd set it loose to starve and die. Johnny came across many of these wayward orphans and always found a place for them.

He whispered some words of kindness in that mare's ear, and she just followed him down the road like a pup, limping along faithfully behind him, for the rest of the day. Long about twilight, they came upon that orchard Johnny was looking for on the Muskingum River, and, wouldn't you know, some settlers had built a cabin right there back of the trees, which had grown up now and were hung with the biggest, ripest, reddest apples anywhere in Ohio.

The man of the house, a big, bearded fellow in buckskins, was busy chopping kindling in the dusty yard, and he looked up when Johnny appeared.

"I bring ye news right fresh from heaven!" Johnny cried out his customary greeting, and at once the pioneer knew who this queer-looking figure he was staring at was.

"Maw, Sara-Jane, Ezra, Isaac, L'il Jasper!" he hollered into the cabin door. "Come on, say howdy-do to Johnny Appleseed!"

And out swarmed the family like honeybees from the hive. They had very few visitors of any kind, being so far from civilization, so a call from Johnny Appleseed was a particular treat, and they got a chance to pay him back for all the fine apples he had given them.

I say they got a chance because it wasn't easy to get Johnny Appleseed to accept anything in repayment, his needs were so very simple. But he did have one weakness, and that was pies.

Johnny wouldn't eat meat, of course, because that would have meant harming some creature. And the truth was, he had a few doubts about the rightness of eating corn, or wheat, or, sometimes, even apples—'cause they were all once living things themselves. But he'd tried getting by eating mud once, and it just wouldn't do, no matter how well he cooked it. So, after that, he generally got along on plain corn mush.

But if a pie happened to show its golden face sailing out from some settler's oven piping hot, why, Johnny could not help himself—especially if it was an *apple* pie! He'd start to twitch and scratch, stretch and scrinch about in his seat.

And if it'd been a specially long interval between pies, his arms might even flap some. Before you knew it, he'd eaten the whole thing. And then he'd ask forgiveness from the Almighty for acting like a darned hog, until the lady of the house said, "But, Johnny, I made that pie just for you. And besides there's another one here for us," at which point Johnny might twitch and scratch and scrinch all over again. But it was his only weakness—pies—and no man is perfect.

By and by, it came time to conduct business. The pioneer family—in this case, name of Huggins, from Fluvanna County, Virginia—they tried to pay Johnny back by giving him a pair of boots, since he was barefoot, and the hard frosts not far off. But he wouldn't take 'em.

"No, sir, no, ma'am," he said. "But I will ask you to take care of this lame spotted horse over the winter for me. And who knows, by spring plowing time, she may be healed up and fit for the furrow."

'Course it was more of a gift than a duty for them, but they promised to treat her like one of the family, and everybody seemed well satisfied to settle accounts.

After that, the little ones were sent off up to their featherbeds in the loft. Johnny'd stay by the fireside and visit with the parents and tell them news from all over. How the War Hawks in Congress were itching to fight the British again. The names of the latest families to settle over by Black Fork, and where they came from. And they might talk about apples some, just when is the time to pick, and how to keep mice from girdling the trunks.

Sometimes, they might ask Johnny how he came to his unusual occupation in life. He'd heave a sigh and drop a fact or two about his boyhood in Massachusetts, and how he'd lost his dear sweetheart to another man and wandered away to the West. But he'd soon get onto his favorite subject, which was the Bible, the Gospels, and his frequent conversations with spirits, and how the Lord had promised him three angel brides in heaven if he stayed pure on earth.

He'd sleep on the floor without a blanket, and the next morning he'd vanish like the dew, leaving folks to wonder if Johnny Appleseed was real or only some enchanted figment they had dreamed about.

Because of his odd appearance and strange ways, the Indians of Ohio took Johnny to be a powerful medicine man and left him alone. He could roam the wildest country without harm. But in eighteen hundred and twelve when war did come, the British sent the Shawnee chief Tecumseh and his warriors on a rampage across the frontier, and Johnny Appleseed ranged ahead of them many a moonstruck night, warning American settlers of approaching danger.

"The spirit of the Lord hath anointed me to blow a trumpet in the wilderness!" he would cry, as he roused the pioneer families from sleep in their isolated cabins, and sent them hurrying off to safety.

By and by, the war came to an end. Life returned to normal on the frontier and Johnny could get on with his main business, which was planting apple trees. After the Shawnee uprisings, the settlers, too, began to believe the rumor that Johnny Appleseed possessed supernatural powers.

One time in Pickaway County, Johnny got word to come cure a sick cow that belonged to a man by the name of Bagley, who owned over a thousand acres. Though he was getting on in years, Johnny walked nine miles barefoot from Circleville to this man Bagley's place in a raw November blow, for it was not in his nature to refuse the needs of a hurt creature.

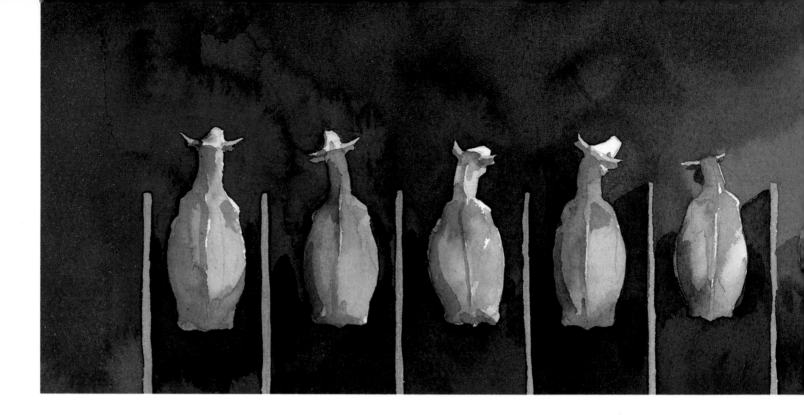

Bagley lived in a new whitewashed clapboard house with real glass windows, and to say he looked well fed was like saying that snakes keep low to the ground.

"It's rumored that you are a hex doctor," he said to Johnny at the front door, not even inviting the old man to step inside and warm himself by the fire.

"I know the natural remedies," was all Johnny said, because he didn't care for these rumors of wizardry that some folks hung on him.

Well, he followed Bagley out to the barn where there was sixteen cows as well fed as their owner, and one bag of bones half-collapsed on the filthy floor of her stall.

"I believe this cow is under a spell," Bagley declared, "and that my neighbor, Clara Potts, has put it on her, for she is a witch as sure as I am a humble farmer."

It so happened Johnny knew Clara Potts, one of the first brave pioneers to cross the Alleghenies. She had a fine orchard of Newton Pippins that he'd planted himself in eighteen hundred and nine. She was a widow now.

Well, Johnny frowned at the rich man in his fine frock coat and then knelt down to see about the cow.

"Fetch me some hay, please," Johnny said to Bagley, who did as he was asked. The cow ate hungrily out of Johnny's hand. "Fetch me a little more, sir," Johnny said.

"Well," said Bagley, "ain't I right? This cow is witched!"

Johnny leaned up close against the sick creature, petted her brow, and whispered something in her ear. And the cow allowed Johnny to enter her thoughts, to read her mind, you might say. Now, whether this was magic or just an extreme sort of natural ability nobody knows, but here is what the cow told Johnny:

"This man keeps me tied up here and will not give me food. Please help me."

Johnny cast another dark glance up at Bagley.

"Say, Appleseed," the squire said, "I want you to testify to what you've seen today. I aim to see that Clara Potts in the Circleville courthouse . . ."

Meanwhile, Johnny helped the cow up on her wobbly feet and began leading her out of the barn.

"Where're you goin' with my cow?" Bagley bellowed.

"If she stays here, she'll die," was all Johnny said.

"Lookit here, Appleseed!" Bagley blustered.

But as he followed Johnny out, why somehow he just managed to step in two milk pails, which caused him to trip over a hay rake, which made him bonk his head on a wheelbarrow—and then the stars came out early for him. Nobody knows if that was wizardry; some folks are just plain clumsy.

Well, it turned out Squire Bagley was after the widow Potts's land, you see, and thought he could bully her out of it. He did see her in the Circleville courthouse after all, but it was at his own trial for telling lies about folks being witches, for which he paid $100 in damages and spent Thanksgiving week in jail. And Johnny gave that cow to a nice young couple who nursed her back to become the finest milker with the creamiest cream of all in Pickaway County, Ohio.

The years rolled and rolled, and Johnny just kept on with his earthly duties of planting apple trees across the frontier. Only thing was, the frontier kept moving west. Ohio was getting downright civilized now, with real towns and stores and folks in Sunday clothes.

So, in his elder days, Johnny Appleseed pushed on to Indiana, still flapping his arms as he marched down the wilderness road, still toting his leather sack of apple seeds, still mad for pies, still saving the lame and the wayward. Until one particular summer evening, he came to the cabin of a young couple on the banks of the Sand River. He gave them the news in exchange for some corn mush and milk, and then, it being a mild evening, he retired outside to watch the sun go down.

Never had the country seemed so beautiful as in the red glow of that evening sun. The stars came out and Johnny begun to imagine they were marvelous constellations of apple blossoms—Sweet Winesaps, Russets, Jonathans, Greenings, Gravensteins, Seek-No-Furthers, American Beauties—until stars and blossoms and fruits all seemed to wheel together in his mind, and slowly, peacefully, Johnny Appleseed went up in the sky among them, to meet his angel brides.